# Heat Wave

*Forbidden Explicit Rough Hottest Taboo Erotic Sexy*

*Short Stories For Adults*

Lana Kendra

it wasn't bought for your personal use only, go back to

your favorite ebook retailer and buy your copy. Thank you

for acknowledging this author's efforts.

# Table of Contents

# Content Warning

Due to its sexual content, this book is only for those over the age of legal adulthood. There are some topics with a lot of foul language. All of the characters are at least eighteen years old.

# Introduction

Are you in search of an exciting and thrilling book to read? Look no further than this extensive collection of Erotic Suspense book. I offer a wide range of genres, including Romantic Erotica, Fantasy, and Urban BDSM Fiction, to cater to even the most discerning reader. Whether you enjoy Anthologies, Westerns, or Paranormal Romance, I have something to suit your taste. My collection also includes Poetic Folklore, Interracial, Black & African American Literary Criticism, and Gothic Horror for those who crave a deeper and darker reading experience. If you're interested in Futuristic, LGBTQ+, Short Stories, or Lesbian literature, my diverse range of options will keep you captivated. Additionally, I offer Humorous, Victorian, New Adult, and College Women's Psychological Mysteries for those seeking a lighter but equally engaging read. Furthermore, My Fairy Tale Collections,

Transgender, Contemporary Western, Bisexual, and Poetry genres will transport you to different worlds and explore a variety of themes. For my Teen and Young Adult readers, I have a selection of European Geography, Cultures, eBooks, Loners, Outcasts, Mythology, Folk Tales, and much more. With such a wide array of options to choose from, you'll never run out of thrilling and enchanting stories to immerse yourself in.

It is important to emphasize that this content is exclusively intended for individuals who are 18 years of age or older.

# Story 1

## Too Hot To Handle

But one evening, though.

My date, Alex, was known, or at least had a reputation for, being highly demanding when it came to intimacy, okay: sex, fucking, so I was really anxious about the date I was getting ready for.

When I saw this man join the line behind me for my morning coffee in the canteen, that's when I first met him. His three-piece suit and tie were well put together, and he had a lovely smile and a well-groomed moustache. Pretty sure she's a little taller than me, with great eyes and clean brown hair. He appeared to have a large chest and, although not being muscular, to maintain a trim figure.

I turned around and grinned broadly, glad to see you. "Hi,

I'm Carol. I haven't seen you here before."

"Pleased to see you as well." He said with a smile that expanded and made me want to know more. His voice gave me shivers. "I'm Alex, I work in Social Services. Don't you work in Town Planning?"

I was flattered that he had any knowledge of me. I might have been more cautious if I had realized that this was the "Mr. Four Ways" Manager of such department, about whom some of the women had laughed.

We got along well and would frequently get together during breaks. Instead of taking me to the canteen for lunch, he would take me out for lunch.

Some other young ladies took notice of this and began making suggestions about him. Such as, "He wants to put it in all four places and is very demanding," which baffled me because I could only think of three. That is, until I recalled a college buddy of mine who categorizes sexual activity as AEIOU. That's Anal, External (for "hand jobs"), Internal, Oral, and Upstairs, or maybe the U for a "titty fuck" that resembles a breast.

Furthermore, "he is a slow burner and will wear you raw," which wasn't too much of a turnoff in my opinion.

It's not fair that 'he probably won't take you to dinner because you don't have much up there,' but the person who said it was clearly a Double D, so that proved it was a titty fuck.

Additionally, "I hope you like saveloys," which are essentially sausages that are significantly longer than average—which I do. My main concern was that they should be "enough," regardless of the term you put in front of them, and certainly nice enough, not the amount of the "sausage" or if they were skinless. As someone once stated, "It's not about the meat, it's about the e-motion," which refers to my current feelings regarding sex.

Now, if we did go on a date—which I really hoped we would—I knew anal sex would most likely—no, definitely—be expected to be involved because I was feeling low on quality male attention and frustrated for reasons I'll describe later. Now since I hadn't done any anal, I talked to my best friend Bella about how to do it. We've been friends since our university courses, so she knows for sure—she's told me plenty of times.

Bella now resembles a sex bomb, and people compare her to myself or nearly any real-life woman. somewhat shorter than I am, but she has an hourglass body and considerably larger breasts, which impresses the guys who aren't put off by her extreme sexiness. her long black hair, big lips, and a gothic aesthetic that was usually accentuated through her clothing. She consistently dons really high heels!

Bella has a wider variety of toys and watches more porn than most males I've met. She also gave me advice on how to prepare for anal sex and train myself. When she gets the chance, she lives in her own apartment, or "lair," with any male who meets her standards for excellence. But most men don't have the endurance she needs, so they only make it across the threshold once.

We frequently venture out to try our luck, but it's not always easy to strike it lucky—especially for me—and most of the time it's more "Wham Bam" than "For the lady's pleasure." I used to frequently hail a cab in the wee hours of the morning for a humiliating journey since I didn't want to wait for more letdown and an identical morning stroll.

I only invited Bella over after I moved into my place if I believed the guys were out. The explanation was that, based on some of her remarks, she thought of them as a buffet bar with unlimited food. I was aware that if given the slightest opportunity, she would have devoured them all at once. I took particular notice of her flirting with Dan. Nevertheless, I trusted her with a backup key in case my own was misplaced while out on the town.

My Great Aunt bequeathed me my home, and those folks were my renters. I observed four men in all, in the sitting room, dining room, and kitchen, but I take care not to intrude into their rooms upstairs. I talked to Dan about my options because I didn't want to rent somewhere in town or evict someone. Dan, who is thirty-three years old, has dark blonde hair that has a noticeable wave, grey eyes, and is undoubtedly the oldest and most experienced of the guys. Measurably taller than six feet, robust physique, and remarkably lengthy digits on small hands. Bella's interest in him made sense to me; if he hadn't been a tenant, I would have been too.

Since the little gym off the lounge already had an ensuite bathroom and a shower, he helped repurpose it, and with his assistance, I moved in. I was ashamed that I had never given him my sincere gratitude, but I also didn't want him to believe that I was making out with him—not that I hadn't thought about it more than once, if not nearly every time I spoke to him.

Even though the boys were all really cute, they were wise enough not to make a move on their landlady, maybe because they weren't sure if it would result in a rent increase or decrease or in eviction. Then, like a child in a candy store who is forbidden from sweets, these are the source of my erotic annoyance.

Aside from their build, height, and hair color, which I will reveal later, I had no idea about their endowment. They had periodically brought back the girls—at first covertly—until I told them I didn't mind if they didn't move in without paying the rent. There didn't seem to be any guests hurrying up the steps just now. It was difficult for me to accept that they didn't have a cleaner because they maintained the common spaces immaculate. They probably didn't want to take a chance on a rent increase, especially after I came in.

Let's go back to Alex. He'd asked me to dinner at one of the local fancy restaurants. Based on previous conversations, I was confident that he would invite me back to his apartment for some fun tonight. Since his department was unrelated to the one I worked in, there was no incentive or pressure.

Since Dan had the master bedroom, I had informed him that I would be going out later and might not return that evening because he always appeared to be up late. It was Friday. Good or Evil? When I returned in my ride of shame, I felt it was thoughtful, and his encouraging comments really lifted my spirits. Thank you, he added, and don't worry, the boys would use the main TV in the sitting room if I was going to be gone and they had some movies to watch.

As I was getting ready, I had a shower, got ready for later, and put on my new underwear, which included a purple push-up bra, thong, and matching garter belt. Derriere's thong was well shown, but it couldn't cover up the "jewel" I had fitted after making my arrangements. After checking the time, I secured the garter belt to my black seamed stockings. Maybe because I was anxious, I turned off the TV and spent some time scrolling through social media while sitting on my bed.

Then it dawned on me that I had left my coat hanging in the front hall, and I looked about for the purple cocktail dress I had purchased on the way home, but I couldn't find it anywhere.

I thought I could just open the door and run to the hall now since my room's door faced the one leading to the hall and cut across the back of the sitting room, but I grabbed my dressing robe nevertheless. I put on the matching high heels since I didn't want to ruin the stockings.

As I ran, I became aware of two—actually, three—realities.

First of all, there was a huge fifty-plus-inch TV that the

guys had purchased on, and three of them were seated in front of it, two on the sofa and one in the armchair to the left, which faced my room. I guess they thought I had already departed.

They had lowered the blinds as well as drawn the curtains because of the TV's placement against the distant wall. I heard voices and faces on the screen, reminiscent of a scene from Friends.

The third was that my dressing gown's belt had come loose. It was a short, silky pink item, so it wouldn't have done much good if I hadn't been holding it closed, which I wasn't.

I heard the distinct sound of a woman being pampered as soon as I unlocked the hall door, stepped inside, and grabbed the bag containing the outfit! I pivoted gradually. The sound must have been coming from the TV as I was positive there were only the three of them sitting there alone.

It was shortly after seven o'clock, and I wondered what my tenants may be watching. Since it wasn't Friends, I cautiously peered around the doorway. I'd seen a lot of Bella's porn, but none with a lady riding a male and holding one in each hand and one in her mouth. Instead of running away, I stood there with my arms by my sides because I was so enthralled.

I saw Ed, who was sitting in the left armchair, his hand down his pants with the belt and button undone. Ed was taller than me, with brown hair cut short. I had a feeling the others were trying to make themselves "comfortable" in a similar way.

I continued to watch as the attractive woman stood up and slid back to sit on the man's face. My left hand had migrated to my thong and was pressing against my mons, but I hadn't recognized it.

Dan's words interrupted my concentration on the screen. He had just emerged from the kitchen door, which faced the sitting room diagonally across from the hall, carrying four bottles of beer. I'm not sure what may have happened.

He always had a clear, calm voice. One of those on the sofa, Francis, was about my age and had curly, ginger hair. "Heads up lads, we have been rumbled, very nicely I may say!" Leaning forward to turn off the TV, someone slightly taller than Dan and with a physique resembling that of a gym devotee heard a lot of whining continuing on the soundtrack.

I stated that in jest. I was mostly kidding, but not lying when I said, "Hey, I was enjoying that, put it back on."

Francis uttered, "Er, it gets a bit stronger next; you might not like it," in a somewhat loud voice.

"Well, I will judge that." I then walked over to the front of the sofa, dropped the suitcase containing my outfit, and took a seat between Francis and Greg. Greg, who is roughly my age and height and has straight brown hair, is an avid rider who frequently wears cycling apparel. He attempted to zip and belt up, but I put my hands on their bulges, which felt good, and they stopped. I knew he had well-muscled legs and a lovely tight butt.

Dan entered in the meantime, set the bottles on the coffee table, and took a seat in the right recliner. He gave me a look, appeared to consider the circumstances, and then said in a steady tone. "All right, let's keep playing the movie, but if we do, just say 'pineapple,' and we will stop the movie and anything else." She directed a sharp glance at Ed, who was still putting his hand down his pants but swiftly took it out. "But I thought you had a date?"

I was so nervous that I couldn't have forgotten. "Oh! Right!" I exclaimed, bolting back into my room, not before hearing Greg, with his thick Scottish accent, declare. "Did you see that in her..." he asked, and if he continued, the sound of the football game on TV would have overpowered him.

My heart was pounding in my room due to the events that had transpired, the idea of four men and me watching porn and other content, the possibility that my preparations would be discovered, and the uncertainty surrounding my date. I was undecided... Bella would know how to handle it. I called her. I squeaked, "Hi, Bel!"

She sounded confident as usual. "Second thoughts about Mr Fourways?"

I made an effort to sound composed. "No, but something has come up here and..."

"You want me to sub?"

"What? No well..."

"Oh." It dawned on me that Bel sounded let down.

"Actually," I said, feeling my heart rush once more as visions of the woman with the four studs flashed through my head. "What are you doing tonight?"

Her voice sounded so innocent, so un-Bel. "What me?" At least Bel was tactless in his candor when he said, "Mostly fantasizing about you and your date... with the aid of Mr. Bunny and some well-hung porn."

"In that case..." I hesitated, unsure of how to phrase my question.

Right on target. "You would like me to take the starring role? It's Alex Hughes, Eight at the Ingenuity Restaurant, right?" I said, surprised at how interested she seemed in the date, but I figured I'd take the chance since Bel wouldn't be upset if I didn't show up.

I was being facetious, but who was I kidding? Bel mind a sure fuck from Mr. Fourways, I didn't know I had done such a wonderful job in sales. "Well, if you don't mind..."

She seemed excited. "Looking forward to it already... yes, just time to prepare myself and get a cab. Enjoy the things that have come up there, and about time, bye." And Bel ended the conversation.

Bel appeared to have read my mind as I stood there in disbelief, and I questioned whether she had a camera in my sitting room. 'Pineapple' never really did enjoy them, to be honest, long breath. Though, sadly, I don't think I will regret this.

I texted Alex, figuring I'd better let him know. I'm sorry, Carol. Please wait for Bella. I'll set my phone on "Airplane" till the morning. I took out my strawberry lubricant and a clear blue dildo to be sure I was sending the lads the right message. I walked in and saw four well-dressed men sipping beer and watching football.

"Ed, pop and get Carol a beer, Francis, get the movie cued up. We have company tonight," Dan replied, clearly indicating that he had seen what I was holding.

As I moved back in front of the sofa and placed the lube

and dildo—one with a sucker on to make it stand up—on the coffee table, the other three gave me a sidelong glance. Afterwards, I positioned myself between Francis and Greg and placed my hands back on their groins, which unhappily no longer had the noticeable bulges that they formerly did.

Dan made a comment and requested. "I take it you have sorted out your date?"

I felt a little guilty, like a mischievous child who has been discovered. "Er, yes, a friend is going with the bad news that, er 'something has come up here'."

"Bella?" he must have asked, judging by the expression on my face. I was shocked that he could recall her name—"really, how could he forget?"—but it seemed that more people were interested in my personal life than I was.

Dan was clearly in charge of this particular occasion. "Right, we all agreed that what happens here will not be mentioned or change anything outside of this room, no favours either way, I hope you agree?"

"Yes, of course, just promise me you will do to me anything they do to the woman in the film."

"Yeah, subject to 'pineapple,' and Greg noticed that you are ready for 'anything,' and you're expecting it," he said, grinning broadly and maintaining an alluring expression in his eyes as he turned to face the coffee table. With that, we were gone. "Francis, press play."

I had no objections, so I reasoned that the conversation must have been quite productive and that Dan might have even established the law.

The woman appeared to be sitting between two males on a sofa at the beginning of the movie; she was wearing a dress and was drinking wine rather than beer. Maybe I should have put mine on, but I didn't want to waste time, so I considered taking Francis's remote control and snogging to the scene where she was in her panties, but it wasn't in reach.

But it didn't take long for her to start wearing only her underwear, with the dress's hem rising to cover her garter belt and the top falling below her breast. However, the men had to remove their cocks! Greg and Francis caught up fast and began snogging me too, with a little hint of a hand on their zips. I felt their hands on my thighs and breasts, their cocks warming up in my palms, and finally their pussy, both inside and outside my thong.

Just as I was getting excited, the main doorbell—not mine—rang. Like the woman on TV, I froze with panic, but Dan just got up and went to the door, and I sat there listening to a conversation that was mumbled, till the door closed.

I was afraid additional boys, or someone new, would enter. Had they invited friends over to give me a Super Gang

Bang? I was hungry right away when I smelled pizza, but I wasn't sure I wanted a full stomach right before sex—or, ideally, getting fucked senselessly.

Dan brought the lube and dildo to the end of the stack of boxes and placed them on the coffee table. In control mode once more. I nodded slightly and said, "Now, what do you want? Let's see we have peperoni." "Hawaiian," I pretended to be serious, but really—"pineapple" on a pizza. "Chicken and mushroom" Almost smiley, but a little too generic. "and Meat Feast?" I grinned broadly since it sounded more like it.

Ed spoke up and glanced at Dan. He laughed and said, "Looks like you have lost your pizza, mate."

I attempted to sound alluring. The four men grinned at that. "Actually, since I am having the full menu tonight," Dan hurried into the kitchen for a few steps, returned with a plate, and dutifully served me. "I'll have a slice of all of them!" I said, adding, "Four slices for me and five for those who have to keep their strength up! And other things." with a pizza.

"As we are talking about the menu, Dan grinned broadly and looked directly at me. If Carol is okay with it, let's watch the movie while we eat to avoid trying to follow along."

With a mouthful of Hawaiian, I said, "Ummm," meaning to remove the least favorite item first. My sensitive spots tingled at the idea of watching a fuck film with four horny men while sipping beer and eating pizza. "Okay, yes, I see the point," I said. "but I want you all dressed like me!"

Greg giggled and arched an eyebrow. "I'm not sure your bras would fit Francis."

Francis guffawed but gave a literal reply in his mind. "I believe she is referring to our underwear," he said, hastily taking off his T-shirt, pants, shoes, and socks before settling down with a wide smile on his face and a bulge in his boxers. The others did the same. Greg was wearing tight-fitting clothing with a prominent bulge oriented to the right; it resembled cycling shorts. Ed's were what I would consider slips, but I imagined mine thong would have a small black spot next to the bulge as well. Dan also had boxers, but they were oversized and showed no signs of bulging, which disappointed me a little.

I started with the "pineapple" then moved on to the chicken and pepperoni while the movie was playing. The two males, "crewcut" and "tattoo," kissed the woman's tits and then her pussy while she massaged their members at the beginning of the movie. After a fight between the two men, one of them threw down his pants, knelt in front of her, tore off his underwear, and drove his head into her mound.

The other man then moved behind the couch and began kissing her, which was nice, but I winced at the forced gagging. He then swung a leg over to allow her to deep throat his cock. As she was pummeling their erections, the original males had managed to get her tits out and were sucking on them. Though my pussy wasn't so sure, I was relieved that we weren't going to attempt to reenact the movie at this point.

When the film cut, the "pussy eater" was lying on his back with his feet facing the camera, and the lady was riding him with a cock in each hand. She moaned in delight, but the "sofa" man quickly forced his cock back into her mouth by holding her head. I winced once more.

Then she stood up, stepped back to sit on the 'pussy eater's' face, then turned around and used assistance to take him up her ass. Her pussy gaped wide open as her ass was pummeled, and she was obviously shaven except for a short landing strip, just like me.

All'sofa man' needed was this to move around and get into her. The camera panned around, focusing on the "sofa man" and the "pussy eater" as they entered and exited while she was being double humped. While "tattoo" was receiving a blowout, "Crewcut" was slaying her tits when he straddled her and proceeded to fuck her tits with a "pussy eater."

I drew a grimace at the 'pussy eater' that was on his back in her pussy after a sudden cut, and the 'crewcut' that was in her ass. She was gagged as 'sofa man' was shoved down her throat in the meantime. Alright, perhaps not everything at once.

After 'sofa man' put his hands around her and 'crewcut' and 'pussy eater' took turns in her ass, another cut and 'tattoo' stood up with his cock in her ass. The other three then took turns in her pussy and ravished her tits. Though I wasn't sure about all the ass and pussy swapping, she seemed to be enjoying it.

After that, they placed her on an Otterman bench, bending

her head back so that they could alternately hold her head and give her a harsh deep throat so that her neck bulged. While this was going on, someone was either in her ass or pussy, and the thought of an ass to mouth didn't appeal to me. When they finally gathered around her, they all shot off covering her lips, tits, and pussy. She appeared to enjoy it, and she definitely earned the money they gave her.

Dan remarked, "OK Smart Speaker, TV off, Play mood music, Lights forty percent," as the credits started to roll.

As I lifted my gaze from the television to grab the last piece of pizza, I noticed that Dan had been staring at me the majority of the time. I almost knocked over the drink when I grabbed it after realizing I was a little shaky, a little frightened, and a lot turned on. Dan grinned, and as he spoke, I paused, the slice halfway to my lips.

"Ed is our ass guy, and once he's in, he's not going anywhere else, I can guarantee you having seen the menu.

When it gets close to the conclusion, no more than two at a time. solely with you in charge of a deep throat. Does that sound right?

I was taken aback; it was as though he had read my thoughts—or maybe just my expression. "Just about and I might even sample some 'pineapple'." I said, giving Ed's Hawaiian a wink and a nod, which elicited some amicable giggles. I was sitting there with the meat feast pizza almost in my mouth when something dripped or fell off onto my breast. I looked down to see Ed licking it off, which gave me a shiver.

Dan grinned and said. "Finish that up and you will start to get a different 'Meat Feast'." And added a big sultry wink. I shook my oily left palm around, and Ed grabbed it and gently sucked it clean. That small act of kindness made me tremble. "I had better nip and wash my hands." I made an announcement and quickly went back to my room to accomplish a little more.

When I got back, I saw that Francis was on the sofa and that Dan and Ed had left. I joined Francis, and he began to massage the part of my breast closest to him. When I turned to face him, he began a passionate kiss, and I unintentionally spread my legs to release the pressure. When Ed returned, he bowed his head right away, pulled down my bra cup, and began to lick and suck at my nipple while sending electric shocks through my body.

Someone pulled me to the edge of the sofa by slipping their hands between my smooth legs. A hand probed my back, feeling for the bra clasp. Reluctantly, I released Francis's firm cock and opened the front clasp, releasing my breasts. I returned to the cock and felt the pre-cum, spreading it with my thumb.

In addition, I was enjoying the attention on my pussy. I could feel the thong being pulled, and just when I thought my suspenders would get tangled, I felt the side bows being loosened. Unexpectedly, that gave me another tingle, though not nearly as much as when my lips were spread by my thumbs and my mouth and tongue were ready to work on me.

I writhed as soon as I felt a small orgasm, especially when their tongue touched my clit. I was hot and eager, and as I bucked up my hips, I realized that Dan had been the one between my legs making sure of it.

Ed's yanking my hand from his cock, which I had just begun to firm, and his abrupt stop of satisfying my achingly hard and tingling nipple somewhat ruined the sensation, but Greg replaced him just in time to restart the stimulation and offer me a fresh cock to fondle. The unexpected cold air felt like a loss as well as a thrill on my vulva. Luckily, it didn't last long since the mouth was back—but this time, it was stronger and more frantic, and it made me tremble. Not that the initial warm-up wasn't something a girl would turn down.

I believed Ed must be there since the idea of his cock in my ass gave me a thrill. Then I felt my butt plug being pulled and adjusted, not enough to move it but enough to intensify my boiling sensations.

I sensed a hand coming over from behind the couch and rubbing my ears and neck. Francis put his mouth against my breast. I looked over and saw Dan smiling broadly, obviously enjoying the sight of me getting pampered to the fullest extent possible. I almost crushed Ed's head with the abrupt intense orgasm that erupted at the mere thought.

"My goodness! Whoah. Very nice.

I turned to face Dan and stated, "I can see and talk now." "Kiss me!" I gasped into Dan's mouth as he leaned over and planted a hard kiss on my back. I responded, causing another surge of pleasure.

The two lips vanished as Dan bent down to caress my breasts. Even though we were snogging, Dan's hands compensated for the loss with a synchronized rotation and nipple tweaking. That triggered a longer, deeper orgasm, during which I arched my back while pressing down on both cocks and used my feet and shoulders as support. I almost crushed them, so I released them and pressed my hands onto the couch instead.

Dan and Ed both stopped kissing as I settled in, but Ed's hands were no longer beneath my ass. I begged Dan to continue kissing, and I saw him nod and look down before he said.

"Ready Babe?" I felt something strange against my lower lip as he called me that for the first time. I looked down and saw Ed kneeling with what appeared to be his cock poised.

"So ready." I returned the whisper, and Dan nodded. Then, I felt Ed's manhood seeping into me, as if he was making sure I was ready—which I was—and he went slowly. I made myself tighten my sex around my pussy when he bottomed out since the progressive filling of my pussy was so erotic.

When Ed reached the tops of my thighs, he started to rub my clit by squeezing my mons around it. He then proceeded to do lengthy strokes in and out of me. I closed my eyes, joy surging inside of me. It wasn't an orgasm; rather, it was more like reaching a new level, and I truly needed hands all over me.

In reality, Francis and Greg had become nude and were kneeling on each side of me, giving their erections to my face after being freed from my grip. I grabbed them once more, this time encompassing the balls that were hanging on Francis but had contracted tightly on Greg, and I began kissing the head of each before moving on to the other, tasting the salty pre-cum.

I took them deeper and deeper with each kiss, reaching as

far as I could with a deep throat, but even so, I felt a tremendous sense of satisfaction from hearing the two men groan. I felt that I needed to learn how to deep-throat from Bella because I was unable to handle them completely.

As all of that was going on, I hardly noticed that Dan had moved away from the guys who were taking control and had stopped massaging his breasts. Ed had intensified his fucking in the meantime, and his thumbs were now right on my clit. I experienced another slow, burning orgasm as my pussy clutched at Ed's dick and my ass on the butt plug. Afterward, he slammed deep inside me, and although I thought I was being filled, it didn't. Then he pulled away, leaving a hole that made me long for its replacement.

I turned to see Dan between my thighs, expecting him to place his arms under my legs and hoist me up so I could land on Ed's stomach, but instead he put his arms under my legs and Greg and Francis lifted me up by the arms. While I lay flat on my back, he turned to rub my breasts with his hand. Francis and Greg knelt down to allow me to caress and then place each of their dicks in my mouth one at a time after I reached up to them.

When Dan elevated my legs, I felt him begin to play with the butt plug. Looking down my body, I could only see Dan's chest.

Dan remarked, grinning, and planted a kiss on my ankle. "Time for this to come out." And with that, he began to rotate and pull at it gradually, building up the force and opening my eyes to the emptiness inside my pussy. I let go of Greg and began to finger myself. When the plug eventually came loose, a weird new climax filled my pussy. The noises were muffled because I was groaning on either Francis's or Greg's cock.

I let some go. "Ohhhh gggoooddd!" Cries when the plug is removed.

I felt Ed's cock round my ass and gently beginning to make

its way in as Dan pushed my knees up to my tits. "Lift me up!" I exclaimed, trying to take charge. With no complaints, Greg and Francis hoisted me up and into a squatting position, with Ed's cock directly in front of my clit. Dan quickly moved off to the side and released my legs. I got up and the guys on either side helped me stay upright until I was able to lower myself onto Ed's cock and put my ass over its head.

The sensation of being stretched was new, even after practicing with butt plugs and a vibrator. Ed's cock molded into my rear entrance, causing me to ease wider and accept the stiff portion of his shaft.

I had never experienced anything like the growing orgasm I experienced as I slowly bounced up and down. I released Greg's cock once more and placed my right hand on my clit, beginning to push it into my pussy and then back up. "I need a cock in me!" Dan was behind me, supporting my shoulders, and he got me to lie back on Ed when I yelled.

Ed began to rock his hips to keep the motions going even though I was having trouble keeping up. My lips spread as I felt my legs hoisted upward and forth. My legs touched Greg's shoulders, and then I felt his cock enter my vagina and my pussy.

I hadn't paid much attention, but he appeared very long and not too wide. I was feeling pretty full at the time, so I started having a huge orgasm when the two men began to alternately move in and out of each other. I groaned since I wasn't gagged with a cock.

"Oh my god, I'm so damn full! "Ahhh."

Greg must have leaned down to suck one of my tits before massaging the other while I was still gripping Francis's cock. My body was trembling when my orgasm struck.

"AAAGHHG! FFFUUUCCCKKK!!!"

And I cried out until Dan's mouth was on mine, inverted, and my body erupted into convulsions as we shared a passionate kiss. My empty hand scrambled to find Dan's penis, but he caught it with his palm and held it tenderly in a reassuring and sensual manner. Dan broke off the kiss as my climax subsided, giving me space to breathe.

Greg's movements abruptly shifted from a steady cadence to a constant deep thrusting, and Ed responded by twisting his hips to maintain the anal pleasure without interfering with Greg's ascending race to an orgasm. He was now banging my clit, and the change in angle felt great, so I didn't worry at all.

I could sense Ed and him both feeling the pressure of my contractions. Suddenly, I felt Greg's sperm splash over my stomach in three or more hot jets, from just above my mons to just below my ribs. He groaned and pulled out.

Francis began to move, and I gave in to his advances without resisting since I could tell where they were going and soon he was beginning to pierce me. Francis's cock appeared slightly thicker than Greg's, but it could have been because my vagina was still convulsing after my most recent orgasm. Greg's cock had been excellent.

As my breathing became labored, Dan knelt down and began caressing my hair and giving me "upside down" kisses. He stopped talking and murmured something in a seductive voice. "relax and enjoy" . I groaned as another climax grew and burst because I was unable to resist.

"Oh my gosh! Ah ah ah!" and so on for a minute or more, my body quivering, twitching, and convulsing; I believe I briefly lost consciousness.

I must have done something to Francis and Ed because they both started to give me the hard way as soon as I calmed down. Another wave of orgasms began at that point, and I felt Francis pull away and shoot his spink all the way up my body, even splattering some on the underside of my tits. My vocal responses were primarily sighs by this point.

"ahhh ohhhh ahhh yesss aaaah yeeessss."

He was hardly done when I felt Ed's cock pulsing in my ass and filling me with his come. This was obviously a novel sensation for me, and it set off a chain reaction that seemed like it was forcing him out of me along with a thrust of my hips. I moved away from Ed's body and ended up next to his perspiring body.

I lay there, fatigued, my eyes fixed on the ceiling light, even though I had done very nothing than get fucked by four dicks and experience what, if you exclude the orgasms from Mr. Rabbit and friends, had been a year's worth of climaxes.

I became aware that there was someone delicately wiping away the spittle all over my body. Dan was squatting next to me, doing a good deed, and I noticed that I was oozing from Ed's anal cream pie as I looked. Dan stood behind me and assisted me in getting to my feet after helping me sit up. After that, I clenched my buttocks and ran as quickly as my unsteady legs would allow. I made myself comfy and enjoyed my post-orgasmic glow by going into my room and ensuite.

# Story 2

## Dark Desire

But for tonight, I'm wearing my red sheath dress, which hits at the mid-thigh and accentuates all of my curves. Sheath dresses are my favorite since they elongate my form, but I also think it looks great on men.

Underneath this are my black fine fishnet stockings, held up by a matching black thong and lace bra. Normally, I wear six-inch heels, but after hearing some advice, I decided to wear four because I want Alex to be able to see my tits. Oh, I forgot to note that the dress had a low back, made possible by the bra, and a plunging neckline.

I also have a treasure for later in my derriere.

arriving on time for the date.

I am running a bit behind schedule for my date with

Alex—well, Carol's date with Alex Hughes—but she called to ask if I could meet him instead because of an unforeseen circumstance. Yes, exactly! Carol shares a home with four eligible guys, Dan in particular, to whom I would never say no. There was just something about him. So, suddenly, right before this wonderful date with Alex, she dithers and calls me. She may have had a better offer recently, and based on her description of Alex, I believe it was a fantastic deal. However, based on all Carol had mentioned about the office gossip about his legendary bedtime skills, I sprang at the possibility, particularly since I was experiencing a bit of a dry spell due to not finding any fresh muffins to entice.

I should probably clarify now that Carol hadn't actually gone on a proper date with Alex—rather, they had just had lunch assignments—and hadn't heard anything about his performance outside of office rumors. He had pursued a number of unmarried women at the Council, all of them willingly and none of them in his Department; nonetheless, the majority of them had concluded that his sexual demands were too demanding for a follow-up date, and none of them had maintained their or his attention for very long.

I was only expecting a single night of pleasure because, in brief, he sounded like exactly my kind of guy. Still, it was better than my plans with Mr. Rabbit, which involved well-hung porn and fantasizing about Carol and Alex.

She had informed me of every remark made about him. I know full well that when a female goes out with a man, her friends find out that he is a porn star on horseback, and that if he dumps her, you need a magnifying lens and a timer. Thus, all of the remarks complimented Alex's skill in using the equipment without disparaging it. He was definitely my ideal man, and it seemed like I wouldn't have to dream about him again.

He was always turned out in a three-piece suit and tie, so Carol couldn't tell me much about his body other than his height of five foot ten inches and his fairly broad chest, but he had a neat and, from the couple of kisses, soft moustache; plus, none of the comments had been negative, like pot belly, so that was a plus.

I had to get dressed quickly and was unable to get a cab until I told the dispatcher, "Tell Tim it's Bella and he can have a special tip if he gets me to the Ingenuity in twenty minutes." Despite my intention to be at the Ingenuity Restaurant by eight, I was not there.

He never wanted more than that, and as a married man, it was more than his wife would be happy for him to receive. Alright, so it meant that I had to give Tim a good sniff, a grope of my tits, and a squeeze of his package, but if that's what it took, then so be it.

The eatery.

Before I head into the restaurant, I touch up my lipstick and make sure my cherry flavor lube bottle's cap is tight.

I will never know quite why Carol had never taken a picture of him, but at nearly twenty past eight, I walk into the restaurant and, ignoring the Maître De, I scan the tables and there he is, elegantly dressed, with the moustache as advertised. I make my best approach through the tables, for hip sway effect, and head for him; he quickly notices my approach, which shows a lively mind, and there's a quizzical smile on his face.

With a seductive smile, I ask, "It's Alex Hughes, right?You can never assume too much.

That's correct, and who do I get to talk to? His tone is friendly and he has an awesome smile."

I extended my hand and stood close to his chair so he could see my body. "This is Bella, Carol's friend, apologizing for her absence."

Nice moustache, must acquire it to tickle my fancy. He examined my body before kissing my hand. "Yes, I received an odd text that said, 'Please wait for Bella, Apologies, Carol.'" When I replied, there was no reply. Could you clarify? And if you plan to stay, kindly take a seat. which, with a wide smile, he answered, "I hope you are."

I bent to give Alex a good look at my cleavage as I sat down opposite him and said, "Yes, she rang me to say that something had come up at home and could I keep the date for her."

"Well, that is very kind of you, but do you know what Carol and I had planned for later?" he said, looking worried but sounding positive nonetheless."

"I am well aware of 'your' plans" I winked, leaning across the table to give him a firm grasp of my nipples, which were beginning to show. "For later and I was very jealous, especially as I had to give her certain derriere training advice." His eyebrows shot up at the word "derriere," and I smiled broadly and winked again.

And Carol won't object if those plans are carried out?And I noticed that, despite his plans to make his date laugh, he was still somewhat concerned, which I found impressive.

With a smile on my face, I said quietly, "Not at all, she would actually be unhappy if she had let you down." Suddenly, my tone completely changed to one of business. "So are we ordering?"

Alex was taken off by this abrupt change of pace for a moment, but he responded extremely gentlemanly: "What would the lady like?"I quickly glanced over the menu and said, 'Well, what I would really like is not on here. And we would get arrested if I had you on the table.'" Then, in a more businesslike tone, I said, "but let's order a couple of sharing starters and some sparkling water as I don't think we want to be bloated or tipsy." He looked puzzled.

The waiter seemed a little confused when Alex quickly agreed, but he continued, saying, "We have a show to get to, but we will come back another night." This sounded promising, and he later said, "I am a bit of a regular in here and they have never queried my succession of dates," which struck me as appropriate. "Ok, you must know what I do, what about you?"

I could see him thinking, "Secretary," "I work for an architect as their structural engineer."

His eyes brightened up and he grinned. "Alex Hughes, Bachelor of Engineering in Civil Engineering, Bristol University." Glad to have met another engineer."

"Bella Ingram, MSc in Structural Engineering, Leeds University." He grinned and did a little bow at my surpassing his degree. I grinned back, thinking, at last, someone on my wavelength.

In our conversation, he disclosed that he was unable to secure employment with a consultant and, in order to make ends meet and cover expenses, took a job in a Council administrative department. Realizing that he was supervising his manager—whose primary credential appeared to be thirty-five years with the Council—he took management training, eventually earning an MBA, bought nice suits, developed a mustache to appear more sophisticated, performed well at work, and continued to receive promotions.

His efforts had paid off, as he was performing admirably at the Council's Social Services Department. His problem-solving and project management skills were highly valued, and he was even referred to as "future Chief Executive material" by some.

I told them I had found my footing because a friend of mine knew that the local Architects were getting tired of paying exorbitant fees for minor structural engineer work, especially when there was a deadline. They decided to give me a six-month contract, and after seeing my work and the help I provided on other projects, they made me a permanent employee halfway through.

There was also the occasion when I was walking past a Partner's office and heard, "future Partner, we don't want to lose her." It might have been someone else, but there were only two other 'hers' in the office and... well, I didn't have the money to 'buy herself in' even if offered. I believe they had discovered that a headhunter hired by one of the other firms that they were now not using was making enquiries.

We spoke during the meal's preparation and consumption, and discovered that while we both enjoyed classical music, finding someone to go to concerts with us proved to be challenging. We also discovered that while hiking in the countryside was enjoyable, most of our joint activities were attended by people who were either retired or shocked to hear that someone 'wanted to concrete over the countryside!' We also agreed that good coffee—that is, not from a pod machine—was essential.

We were going to depart within an hour, and Alex offered to take me to his place, but I have a policy of'my place or no place,' so we settled the bill and he wouldn't hear otherwise.

He quickly advanced further in my opinion by stating, without hesitation, "The lady's wish is my command."

Alex's car was parked around the back and we headed to my flat, which is above a high street shop with no other flats above it at the moment (though my firm are working on that). As a result, I enjoy complete privacy after closing shop time.

After we entered, I shut the door, hung up my coat, took off my shoes, and embraced Alex, giving him a passionate French kiss that he gladly returned, his hands scurrying up and down my back and cupping my buttocks.

He slipped off both of his shoes, so I ran my hands down the front of his shirt and felt a lovely, firm, but not too muscular torso. I put my hands in the front of his jacket and slid it off his shoulders and he extended his arms to allow it drop behind him.

My pulse was pounding with the excitement of the upcoming night, and even though I knew I didn't have to seduce him, I wanted to nonetheless. I said in a sultry voice, "Follow me." and made my way to my bedroom with its king-sized bed.

I was impressed by his smile when we entered my boudoir, which was already sensually lit with mood music and had the duvet rolled down to the foot of the bed. I pushed him onto the bed, where I climbed onto him and he undid his shirt while we kissed and he fondled my breasts, getting my nipples to respond nicely and giving me a tingle in my groin.

I undressed his shirt, revealing his toned, lightly tanned chest with unusually erect nipples. I properly kissed and licked them, eliciting a small groan from him, and felt movement in his pants as I sat on him.

Alex instantly rocked back and lifted his hips so that I could whip his trousers off in one movement, including his socks, and he sat there in just his boxer shorts looking at me with lust-filled eyes and a prominent and promising-looking tent. I slid back to stand between his legs, unbuckled his belt, released the waist of his trousers, and lowered the zip.

It was pure coincidence that the next song was a slow, sensual saxophone track, so I swayed to the music, turned my back on Alex, crossed my arms, and leaned forward to grab the bottom of my dress, pulling it up and over my head in one long, slow motion. Okay, I like it when a man does it, but sometimes the impact of a seductive reveal is more significant.

Alex took a breath, which thrilled me, and then said a hushed "Wow" and "Bella, where have you been all my life?I turned to face him as the music went on and moved my hands all over my body.

His smile expanded and I saw his boxers becoming even more tensed as I replied, all sex in my voice, "Let's make up for lost time."

With a hopeful smile, Adam added, "Maybe a lap dance would be fun?"

"Oh, you are an expert in getting those?" I mocked him."

With a huge smile on his face and a twitchy tent, he said, "Not at all, ever, but it sounds like an opportunity to get my hands on your beautiful body." Despite his boxers and my thong, I couldn't wait to feel the tent against my pussy.

Turning around, I delicately lowered my legs to straddle

Alex's, putting his dick between them. As I nestled in, I felt the shaft make contact with my clit and labia, which sent a surge of ecstasy through my body while I continued to dance to the music.

I craved contact, so I slowly got up and started rotating my arse cheeks in his face while I reached back and untied my bra. I felt his hands caress my bottom and then a tingle as he shoved the gem in my butt. Alex's hands came around me and cupped my breasts and tickled my nipples through the lace.

I turned to face him and dropped the bra straps in his lap, saying, "These are your treat at the moment." He took them gently and tweaked and sucked my nipples until they were bigger than I had seen them in a long time, and it created a type of orgasm that I had not felt before. I shook and let out a long moan of pleasure. I reprimanded him gently. "Naughty boy, that's a treat later for a good boy."

"Alex, you're so incredibly talented. Oh no! So really good.

Then, with a flourish, I turned and made the big reveal of my already very damp and well-trimmed pussy, with just a landing strip above my engorged labia and waiting clit. Reluctantly, I released myself, turned, and loosened the side ties of my thong, dropping the rear.

Alex was obviously about to pounce as I used my fingers to widen my sex and expose my clit to his very ravenous vision. I reached down to his boxers, which had a very damp place at the top of their inflated bulge.

I gave him a growl and said, "Now it's your turn!"and he reclined, lifting his hips to allow me to remove them, revealing his erection for the first time.

I could tell right away that his dick was long and fairly broad, and that the top third of his shaft was free of his foreskin, which made it look so much nicer than those that merely peep—not that those don't fulfill me in the proper hands, but just look at it!

I just had to have a lick of his sex lollypop, and it, and the pre-cum, was delicious. His balls looked nice, tight but still with some fondle room, and similarly shaved. He obviously took care to groom himself, as evidenced by the hair being clear of the base of the shaft and the absence of excessive musk from neglect.

"Right you! " said in a Mistress Whiplash voice. Move to the center of the bed!"It's okay, I like the taste of cum, and Alex provided both quality and quantity. I quickly obeyed, chasing him while laying down facing his hips to better deep throat him. I leaned over and lifted his dick with my right hand, taking my tongue around the crest of his glans and savoring the remaining pre-cum.

I dropped my hips lower to make his contact easier, without suffocating him, though his expert mouth work ensured I would never want to do that. I had planned to give Alex the deep throat while he lay there and possibly fingered me, but he gently lifted my knee and swung his head under my pussy and raised his head to run his tongue tinglingly along my folds.

I like to give deep throats when I am in control and can get the pleasure I want out of them. Head gripping and tea bagging are not in my repertoire. With that, I slipped his dick down my throat and rocked back and forth to achieve a thrusting motion.

Alex's right hand was playing with my left tit and the engorged nipple, while his left was playing with the butt plug and swirling it nicely. While I was doing this, his tongue was deftly rimming my vagina and his chin was massaging my clit. I was also playing with his rather nice balls with one hand and massaging around the base of his cock and his pubic bone with the other.

He then brought his right hand back, and I raised my thighs

to relieve some pressure on his jaw while he worked two fingers into my wet vagina and his thumb rubbed my clit, causing tremors in me. I realized that his fingers were rubbing my front wall in an attempt to find my g-spot, which was evidently causing my vagina to convulse and give me an orgasm. My only recourse was to push him back of my throat and massage his balls; I would have made more noise, but a dick in my throat meant that it was only a hum.

"aaahhhooohhhaaahhh ah ah aahhhooohhhaaahh"

I quickly opened my mouth to catch his yummy spunk, but then his hips moved as if he was cumming, which wouldn't have surprised any other man, let alone one with Alex's, 'Mr Fourways' reputation.

He settled down and then redoubled his efforts, and was rewarded by delivering me another orgasm, deeper and harder than the first; in the meantime, his erection remained, if anything, stronger and hotter than before, with no indication of it withering. But all I got was an excessive amount of pre-cum leaking out.

I lifted my hips to allow Alex to continue speaking during my orgasm. He said, "I would love to see your breasts and make love to them." In a voice so seductive that any girl would have to be incredibly heartless to refuse, so I rolled onto my back and awaited his next move, but not before grabbing the cherry lube bottle.

Alex sat up, turned around, and straddled my chest just under my tits and laid his dick between them. I quickly applied some lube and pressed the head down to lie flat so that he could wrap it by squeezing them together like a very hot, hot dog. I had my head towards the foot of the bed, with it resting on the folded duvet.

As he rocked back and began to thrust, I was able to get my lips in a position where I could kiss the glans as they kept peeking out and taste the combination of his pre-cum and cherry. He began to rock back and forth and used his thumbs to gather some lubrication, which he applied to my nipples, making them tingle and engorge.

He was taken aback when I touched his chest and caressed his nipples, but he grinned as they stood proudly. I had also gotten some lubrication on my fingertips.

He inquired in between thrusts, "Can... You. ponder... pause... out of... You're... itts?"And since it allowed me to play with them myself, I readily replied.

I bent my legs up so that I could rotate my hips up to give him renewed access to my vagina, and again two fingers entered and massaged my g-spot. What. A. Man! Alex then took his left hand and gently held on to my shoulder to enable him to trust more vigorously. He then brought his right hand behind him and onto my pussy so he could still massage my labia and clit.

Although some women find titty fucks uncomfortable, Alex made sure I was completely engaged. His g-spot abilities and my ability to produce a true thrill or perhaps an orgasm made me feel like a bucking bronco in no time.

"OHHH FUUUUUCCCCKKKK! ALEXXXX YOU ARE SOOOO FUCKKKING GOOOOOD! FUUCCCKKK AHHHH!"

If you can call the copious pre-cum dry, I believe my satisfaction propelled Alex over the edge with a loud groan, but for him it was just another weird dry shudder.

Whatever it was, it made Alex fall off me and onto the bed, his head almost resting on the foot. I rolled over in order to yank him into a more comfortable position and engage in a frenzied French kissing session with him.

My right hand drifted to his hard, pulsating dick, where I played with the frenum—a web of nerve-rich skin that runs on the bottom of a dick between the glans and the saft—and gently moved the foreskin up and down. Alex moaned with delight at my focus. His left hand attempted to rub my clit by climbing up my thigh and searching for my mons.

I softly murmured in his ear. I tugged at his erection, telling him, "Enough play, time to put this." "where I have a hot home waiting!"

He gave me a smile, and between the two of us, I ended up lying on the bed correctly, with one cushion under my head and the other under my hips. I instantly wanted Alex's dick in me as he sat between my knees and grinned so seductively at me that it gave me chills. I opened my sex to him by spreading my stockinged legs.

The ecstasy of the contact was overshadowed by the need for penetration as he leaned down and placed his hands on my thighs and his tongue on my pussy. My legs shot straight up as soon as he stuck two fingers inside of me and made contact with my g-spot once more. This instantly caused an orgasm.

"AHHHH SOOOO GGGOOOODDD, ALLLEEEXXXX BBBUUUUTTTT PPLLLEEASSE FFFUUUCCCKKKK MEEEE!!!"

Alex rapidly rammed his erection into my eager body by bringing them up against his chest and over his right shoulder. He then raised me onto my shoulders. I couldn't tell if that was a new orgasm or just a continuation of the previous one. Alex appeared fixated on giving me pleasure, so he partially withdrew and gave me a brief thrust that struck my g-spot.

He withdrew and continued doing the same, endlessly, as I screamed like a banshee, cursed, and swayed my tits. Like I was in an orgasmic earthquake rather than a quake.

"OHHH FUCCCKKK, FUUCCCKKKKING GOOODD FUUUUCCCKKKKIIINNNG FFFUUUCCCKKK!!!"

Alex had a huge smile on his face, and I could see that he was really attracted to my orgasms.

I swallowed and tried to talk normally, but I was begging him with all my might. "Fuck me... Fuck me now... Fuck MEEEE!" I felt a sensation throughout my entire body that I had never had before. When he eventually penetrated me to the point where his wonderful shaft touched my cervix and his pubic bone struck my clit, he let me to drop off his dick and return to the bed, where I opened my legs again and Alex laid over me. However, I observed that the head of his dick was quite wet.

I let out another scream and encircled my body around his back, bending at the ankles.

"AAAAAAAAGGGGGHHHH!!!!"

After that, he began to drive long, hard strokes into me, rotating his pelvis at the end of each to massage my cervix and clit. Additionally, my very sensitive g-spot continued to be stimulated. He was standing on his arms, but he was bending down to give me a passionate kiss. I gave him back the kiss and ran my hands over his chest, playing with his nipples. I was willing to make the sacrifice, even if it was nearly too much for a girl to handle.

After that, he arched his back, lowered his mouth to my right breast, sucked it in, and gently teased my nipple with his teeth while playing with it with his tongue. Another orgasm erupted, and I was conscious that his rotations were stimulating my anus and butt plug as I wriggled and rocked.

Then, with a pop, he raised his head, released the teat, and dove onto his left breast to accomplish the same thing. and I bucked my hips one more as I came. I let out a yell.

"OH MY GOD! AHHHHh! OHHHh! AGHhhhh! AIaeeee! AH! Ah! ahh. FUCKKK! Fuck! fuck..."

And so it continued, powering in and out as my vagina

continued to contract on his manhood.

Alex started grunting and ramming in and out, nothing fancy, just long strokes at first. He also raised his head, not kissing or playing with my tits, just staring down at me while my tits flailed around, continuing to feed my chain of orgasms.

He thrust his dick hard and collapsed on my chest, letting out a sudden roar. I felt his dick surge and the distinct warmth of his come striking my cervix. He groaned repeatedly, filling my vagina with his seed.

He rested gently on my right shoulder, his head resting on me, and I lost count after four or five large spurts.

I let go and dropped my legs since they were tired and ended up flat on his side of the bed.

As we lay there, gathering our strength, I became aware that Alex was crying softly. As I turned to kiss his cheek, I noticed it was wet.

With a hint of worry in my voice, I muttered. "Hey, hansom, big boys don't cry."

He gave me a kiss on the lips with a turn of his head that, for some reason, was much more sensual than our earlier kisses.

He seemed confused. "Sorry, that was wonderful, and I have never come in a woman before."

That confused me until I understood that he was referring to my vagina. It didn't seem possible that he had only ever used his anal, or as he later clarified, frequently as a hand job when the date could handle no more.

I recognized he was in need of some motivation, so I said. "Hey, that was fantastic, you are the best lover I have ever had, and I have tried a few. Nothing to be sorry about."

After that, we shared another passionate kiss, this time interspersed with glances at one another. Even though Alex was still hard in my vagina, I could still feel a tingle in my vagina as we moved because it seemed like it had done its job of keeping me spunky.

I realized that Alex had missed an area as we lay side by side. I wasn't complaining because I still had my butt plug in, but I also wanted a coffee.

So I enquired, as though we weren't nude and he wasn't in my pussy. "Cappuccino?"

Alex simply nodded, his smile having taken the place of his sorrow. He rolled over to face my leaving body as I stood up, and he gave me a short pat on the back as I hurried to the ensuite to deal with the fallout from our passionate encounter.

After I left, he peeked in, and I quickly grabbed my silky, short dressing robe and wrapped it about myself. Alex, who was wearing boxer shorts, approached me from behind as I was standing in the kitchen area off the lounge, where my fancy auto barista machine was grinding, brewing, and adding the perfect amount of steamed and frothed milk. His dick was stiff and sitting in the space between my butt cheeks, and I couldn't help but notice that.

He tenderly put his arms around my waist, placed his head on my right shoulder, and gave me a quick kiss on the neck. He stated in a matter-of-fact manner while glancing at the machine at work. "I do my own grinding and steaming."

Sexily, I answered. I could feel his smile and the surge in his dick, but he didn't reach for my breast or pussy, which was lovely and flattering. "Yes, I have noticed... and very good you are at both." I raised my hand to the shaker and said, "Chocolate?"

Talking as if we were in a coffee shop. "I'd prefer cinnamon if you have it?"

I laughed sexily at him. He handed him the smaller shaker from the back of the store and said, "Ohh, very conservative for one who beds young maidens at every opportunity."

Taking our drinks, we sat at the 'breakfast bar' side by side, with Alex's left arm over me.

Alex gave me a squeeze in reprimand. "I'd have thought you would have taken the traditional option."

My voice, though, was dripping with sensuality. But Alex didn't follow up on it. "I was seduced by the treat at the end... of the drink." As we drank, continuing from the restaurant as if Alex hadn't just thoroughly and truly rode me for the better part of an hour and given me many orgasms, we talked about work and interests.

I also thought to myself that I had given him an orgasm that was really precious to him, and I hoped that was me. Though I was curious about his focus on my g-spot, I wasn't unhappy.

I moaned as I put a dollop of chocolate-covered froth in my mouth after we completed our coffee and reached for my spoon. stated Alex. "That does look nice."

I gave a cheeky reply. I dropped the next mouthful on my left breast after realizing my dressing robe had gaped open, hearing her say, "You should try it." I made him laugh. "Oh dear, you will have to lick it off me to taste it."

With a grunt, he grinned. And he leaned over and sucked it off, saying, "Don't mind if I do." He said, "Oh dear, I have missed a bit." I have to admit that I didn't think he had, but he turned around, pushed the robe aside, and lifted my tit to give me a kiss before sucking my nipple.

I turned to face him, and while I was giving him a nice hand job, my left hand reached across and wrapped around his still-erect dick. Alex, in the meantime, had turned to face me, his left arm scouring through my robe for my pussy.

I ended the kiss and pretended that we were in a meeting. Without saying anything, I led him back while holding hands in front of me, saying, "I think we had to take this back to the bedroom. You have unfinished business, Mister." We were not going to follow his four ways script anymore, so when we went to the bed, I decided I wanted to be in command.

More tone of Mistress Whiplash. "Right Stud, lie on the bed, which way do you like your cowgirl, forward or backward?"

Alex leaped enthusiastically onto the bed and answered. "Forward, of course, I don't want to miss those luscious tits."

"Forward it is then!"

Then, he pouted, his expression reminiscent of a small boy. Who was I to refuse him that, given how skilled he was at making me feel good with his mouth? "But first, can I have another taste of your sexy pussy?" he said.

Alex took off my dressing gown while I positioned myself,

then wrapped his arms around my ankles to reach up and stroke my breasts from the sides. I placed my mons on his face, bringing his nose to the base of my sex, and I used it to spread my lips and rub my clit.

Naturally, he quickly turned his head back to use his lips and tongue, pressing his chin against my perinium while attempting to penetrate and rim me with his tongue.

After raising my nipples with his hands, he moved the left one down to play with my buttplug once more, swishing and twisting it to enhance the feelings that flooded into my lips and clit. Not surprisingly, my vagina was itching for something to fill it, so I came and came hard, bucking and trembling and almost choking Alex.

Alex skillfully turned his right hand around as I was standing up and managed to put three fingers into my sex, but he was unable to massage my g-spot because it was facing my back wall. Nevertheless, he was able to flex his fingers and apply pressure, which made me scream because it was still extremely sensitive. I leaped skyward, leaving his fingers behind.

"AHHHAAHHH!!!! Enough, enough, I need your dick, I need it now!"

And Alex helped me to lower myself slowly onto his wonderful erection by supporting my hips as I slid back over his pelvis. My vagina continued to spasm around it as it filled me, but now that I had something to squeeze, the anguish turned into an ecstasy.

I could begin moving up and down on him, the glans sliding from g-spot to cervix, once I was well inserted. I felt that Alex had lubricated his fingers as he reached up and began to play with my tits, rubbing and adjusting my nipples. My next orgasm was rapidly approaching thanks to all of this stimulation.

"OHHHH     AALLLEEEXXX...     FUUUCCCKKK!

HHOOLLY                    FUCKKKKIIINNGGG

FFFFUUUCCCCKKK!!!"

I saw the expression on Alex's face as I shouted and shook; he trembled too, and his dick surged with another of his semi-orgasms.

Alex supported me in reclining and raised his hips a few inches while I regained my composure. After getting into position, he quickly began to thrust his pelvis up and down. Because of the angle and height, he put more pressure on my g-spot than before and continued to nub my clit and cervix. My engorged nipples seemed to have a life of their own, and my tits were free to flutter around while his hands supported my bottoms, providing their own unique sensation.

Needless to say, I had to lean forward to collapse on Alex's chest and smother his mouth with ravenous kisses as another orgasm mounted quickly.

"Aaaalllleeexxxx. Sooo Goood. Toooo Goood."

He continued to pound away and maintain my hips up, but he did so with less pressure on my g-spot. This continued my orgasm, but eventually my body contracted so hard that Alex's dick was forced to let off of my hips or risk having it ripped off! He put his arms around me and massaged my back from my buttocks to my neck, and I felt he had another semi.

Though it might not be to every girl's taste, I wanted to try Alex's fourth way—being ready, experienced, and with a partner who I knew would know how to make it enjoyable—rather than just lying there in his arms.

I whispered in his right ear in my sexiest voice. He nodded, obviously having heard the title before, and I felt his hand slip behind me to gently grab the jewel. "Ready, Mister Four Ways?" he asked. He swirled it and applied more and more pressure till it was almost out, at which point he let it slip back partially and then out once more.

He was skilled at what he was doing, and as the pleasure increased, my muscles there relaxed. He was able to repeatedly bring the widest point out and back, and I felt my contractions flow out of sympathy. I then massaged Alex's dick, which caused him to sigh once more.

I slowly stood up, and as he withdrew the plug with his hand, I smelled hot cherry lubricant. After standing up, I raised my body to the point where Alex's dick emerged from my pussy, then I reached down to position him on my ass.

I had refilled my ass lubricant so that as I lowered myself, his dick made contact and then glided effortlessly through the opening. Since the sensitivity is there, I just took him a few inches in. After that, I leaned back and braced myself by placing my arms on his legs.

As Alex rubbed my clit with his right thumb and

alternatively tweaked my nipples with his left, I could feel my labia flexing open and shut. I started to ride up and down to get the stimulation in both my ass and my pussy. I continued the action for a few minutes as my orgasm intensified. I froze and got up when it shattered since it was the best of that kind I had ever had.

"Ahhh Alexxx! You fiillll me up soooo wweeellll!"

Alex then began to twist his hips in order to keep his dick in my ass and massage my clit and vaginal opening with both of his thumbs. His trust continued to grow, creating yet another enormous climax. I yelled with delight, my head turned to the ceiling.

"SSHHHIIIITTTT!!!"

I felt his hot spunk rush into me and could imagine the smile on his face the last time he orgasmed, even though I couldn't see it. I leaned forward and nestled on Alex's warm chest, enjoying the sensation of his rise and fall and the pounding of his heart, till his hips gave out after another six thrusts.

Alex got me to slide off him just as I was ready to nod asleep, then reached down and pulled the blanket over us. I believe that, for the first time in my life, I was infatuated with a man's body as well as his soul; yet, I chose not to consider the possibility of life after tomorrow. It's likely that Alex was unaware that he would be among the select few who would awaken in my bed.

stated Alex. With the exception of our breathing, all was dark and silent when we heard the command, "Smart Speaker, light off, music off." Perhaps for the first time in many, many years, I felt strangely joyful and content as I curled up against him and quickly fell asleep.

# Story 3

## The Missing Partner

Carol returned to her room.

Having been willingly fucked by four men—including my first anal and double penetration experiences—I was well and thoroughly shagged.

Watching a similar incident on a hard porn video while sitting in skimpy underwear with a cock in each hand and two men's hands caressing my tits and pussy had really made me crazy. The woman on the video appeared to be having a great time most of the time, but Dan—who was a little older—seemed to be making sure that I had the best possible time in real life. Pineapple was a safe word, so I could kick back and enjoy the ride. What fun, too! With the exception of orgasms from vibrators, I had experienced more orgasms in those few hours than I had in the previous year, and that was a close call.

After returning to my room, I thought I should take some time to relax and bask in my post-orgasmic glow.

Then I noticed the time and began to wonder. It was only a little after half nine in the evening, and without a warm body to cuddle with, the orgasmic glow was quickly dissipating. And then I thought, maybe instead of hiring my best friend Bella to cover for me, I could have kept my date with Alex, aka Mr. Fourways, enjoyed a beautiful supper and his attentive attentions.

I couldn't help but notice another thing—four men, four cocks—but didn't I already have Ed's twice? Then I realized that I had left my butt plug in the living room and that I was still wet where Ed had touched my behind. I fingered my clit in an attempt to calm myself, but it only made me feel more uneasy.

I got up as I was starting to feel uneasy, carefully made my way to my door, opened it a little, and peered out into the living room, where music was softly playing and the light was still on but had dimmed. I went to get my dressing gown and abandoned thong because it appeared to be deserted and I was hoping to discover the butt plug. No matter how well-prepared I was for the back door experience—which I had never really had in real life—a DP and four men's attention can do that to a woman, so I walked a little bow-legged.

When I reached the spot where the thong and gown were laying on the ground, I bent over to check below them, only to find that the butt plug was missing.

A seductively taunting masculine voice enquired. It was coming from the couch behind me and I knew it was Dan's voice asking, "Looking for something?"

When I looked at his face and realized I had been mooning

and pussy flashing him, I instantly smiled back, without even trying. He had a big semi-erection, which I didn't recognize from my small orgy earlier, and was somewhat reclined on the sofa. He also had the butt plug. And I would have known that it was larger and, unlike the others, circumcised, but maybe it was just wishful thinking. I was aware that I hadn't had any pleasure from it, and most definitely not in my pussy.

I moved forward, removed the plug from his uncooperative fingers, and hesitated before replacing it.

Dan reassured everyone, saying, "It's okay, I've lubed it."

I leaned closer to give it more ease and to see more of his masculinity, phallus, cock, and erection. Whoa, I was practically drooling, and not from my mouth alone.

Placing my hands on my hips and opening my legs wide, not just my legs, I inquired in a seductive voice, trying not to sound like I was making a slight accusation, which I kind of was. "Didn't you want to fuck me?"

The sound of Dan's voice made me tingle right away. "I've wanted to make love to you from the day you moved in. No, tell a lie. From the moment you introduced yourself to us as our new landlady."

With a tinge of regret in my speech, I wondered whether I had ruined things with him by being a bit of a trollop. "So why didn't you join in?"

I sat right up next to Dan, making as much body contact as possible, and turned to face him as he swung his legs down to sit up and patted the couch next to him. He patted my jaw and muttered something quietly just as I was ready to inquire again. "I could see you were turned on by the idea of having multiple partners. But it's not how I wanted to experience you... or us."

It baffled me. I said with a gleam of hope, "But you were there, you kissed me, aroused me, and ate my pussy." "You looked after me?"

Dan has such a comforting voice. "Yes, that is what I was doing. If I had left, possibly the boys would have got too excited and spoilt your experience."

I tried not to seem worried, even though a sudden notion made me fear that this moment would not go as planned. "About them, where are they?"

"Gone to bed, you wore them out, and they have to be up early to get a coach to the footy. Away game," said Dan, grinning and stroking my jaw to calm me.

"And you?" There must have been a hint of concern in my voice.

Dan shot me a broad, seductive smile. "No footy plans," which turned out to be untrue. Another shiver of expectation went through me, "hopefully something much better?" He reached forward to plant a comforting kiss on my lips.

I smiled broadly at him and felt a surge of exhilaration. "Like what?"

Dan got up and extended his hand to me. It was then that I foolishly noticed that his growing cock, which was the largest I had ever seen, was concealed in his lap for a good few inches. "Oh, my heart, please stop beating!" Actually, no... Hurry up and get moving!"

He said, as I stood. He really knocked me flat when he said, "Let's discuss this somewhere more comfortable." But instead of going to my room, he carried me upstairs to his room, where he placed me down on his king-sized bed and gave me constant, passionate kisses.

With such tenderness in his voice, he inquired, "Comfy?" after having just deposited an almost nude woman on his bed. I was more of a sit, with my elbows behind me to allow me to glance around, and my legs bent with my knees together.

Although I had never been in this area before, I was taken aback by how nice and orderly it seemed—not at all like the run-down mancave I had imagined. Fresh laundry smelled in the room as well. I couldn't help but notice the occupant's charming manhood, which caught my attention.

"Very." I answered, and he slipped between my legs, which I spread out before deciding to recline. But before I could ruin the moment, I saw that my stomach was sticky from the guys' climax as I was about to totally expose my breasts by putting my hands behind my head.

I thought Dan was going to fuck me or at least lick my pussy when he leaned between my legs, but he stopped short of that. I briefly had rejection panic.

But he followed it with a gentle patting of his left hand and then his lips as he released the top of my right stocking and rolled it off my leg. I experienced a shiver and a twitch in my pussy.

With my left leg, he did the same thing again, but this time he began with a tiny kiss on top of my expanded labia, which I could feel opening at his touch.

Dan's hands were dainty for a man, with long fingers and a gentle touch, and when he reached to take off my suspender belt, he saw that it was adhered to my skin with dried sperm.

When it broke loose, he elevated my butt, and I had to lift my legs and close them to allow him to remove it, exposing me completely. I was ecstatic to realize that Dan was going to make love to me. Not just a sexualized version of me, like the boys had just done, but just me. I felt tingles run down my spine, and I was ready.

I opened myself to him by spreading my legs wide again, exposing my clit with my right hand, and closing my eyes to wait for his touch.

I was taken aback when Dan got up from the bed, picked

me up once more, and carried me into the bathroom, where he stood me in the spacious shower cabinet at the end of the tub. He turned and left! "Oh no, he doesn't want me and is embarrassed that I am dirty!"I took hold of his hand.

I begged in a seductive, maiden in distress voice. "I'm not familiar with the controls; is there any way you could help me?" I asked, and with the tiniest gesture, he came to join me. After that, I kissed him.

Dan put his hand behind my head as I leaned forward to kiss him, and our tongues began to dance as we had a full-on snogging session. He gestured to the control and talked in a matter-of-fact manner, but he also included a hint of humor as we split up.

"Two buttons: the shower head's dial temperature and the outer ring water." "shower pattern." He winked broadly, confident that I was aware of that from the beginning. But it was obvious that he was sticky now as he pulled away from me. "Oh dear," he said in a mocking terror tone. "I need to take a shower too!" followed by a sly grin. "Will you soap me down?"

With a seductive growl and a beaming smile, I said, "Try and stop me." Then, I turned on the water and began to run a soft flow between us. Dan used a tiny bit of shower gel on his palm to delicately massage my 'landing strip'—the area between my breasts and the top—without accidentally soaping my pussy.

I responded by stroking the same spot on Dan with my hand, not stopping where he did, but instead continuing to slide my moist, non-soapy palm over his raging cock. His ball sack had contracted into a substantial yet solid bulge between his legs, which caught my attention. In addition, I saw that he had combed his pubic hair back from his balls and shaft.

After he turned me around, he removed the butt plug. "You

don't need that; just clench three times and I'll rinse you down." With that, he turned on a mild flow in the shower and 'hosed' me down, creating a seductive effect. However, I obediently clenched my buttocks three times, and then perhaps five more.

Dan whispered as he rested his head on my shoulder and used one hand to massage my breast. "Much as shower sex is nice, I think what I have in mind will be nicer."

He turned off the shower, led me out of the booth, and began drying me from the back down. I was astounded by the towel's whiteness and smoothness, and he followed it down with tender kisses. He dried between my buttocks, kissing them and my upper thighs, then gently widened the space between my legs. I felt like a sexual goddess being worshipped because of his tenderness, which was a huge turn on.

He spun me around and did it again, but this time, after

giving me a little snooze, he began with dry kisses on my nipples and worked his way down, covering my navel and ending at the top of my pussy. His nose tickled my clit and almost made my legs buckle as he licked my inner thighs. Dan gulped, raised his head, and grinned.

"That smells so nice." He quickly licked his mouth.

"And tastes nice." At that point, my knees buckled, so he wrapped his arms around my waist and supported me while I stood up. He cleaned himself off quickly and took me to the bed, where he placed me down and rolled me to lie down the center, flat this time, calm and waiting, till my legs were dry enough to kiss my feet.

Then Dan moved up my body until he was fully extended, and we had a passionate French kiss. I'm not sure how his cock managed to stay out of my vagina on its own, but it felt amazing resting along my lips where it stroked my clit and began to build up to a full-blown, silently groaning orgasm that left me drenched and panting.

After rolling onto our sides, Dan reached down and caressed my pussy, bending over to kiss my left breast and running his fingers over my lips with his right, while his other hand caressed my right and teased my nipple. He slowly inserted one finger, then two, then three into my eager sex.

Working them gently deeper, then rotating them and pressing my curled fingertips up against my vagina's front wall. I let out a small gasp as his touch passed over a certain region. Then he moved them back, and Dan started caressing me in a new way that made me have yet another orgasm. Finally, he added a lightning-bolt of his thumb contacting my clit and rolling over it, which made me scream.

"AHHAGH DAAANNN, HOOLLLYYY FFUUCCKKKING FUCK!!!"

And bucked and trembled in an orgasm I had never known, and I believed I would pass away a contented and worn-out woman.

When my senses returned, I realized that I had not been completely passive because my right hand was cradling Dan's enormous cock—my hands would have remained full even if I had been using two hands. I ran my hand over the considerable quantity of pre-cum that was dripping out of the tip of his amazing member. I pulled out of his grip and lowered my head to suck on his gorgeous cock as I healed, if I would ever completely heal.

Dan felt through my hair. His voice was so sweet, sensual, and alluring. "That is so nice, but I think you have a better place for both of our enjoyment." .

I extended my legs wide on my back and brought them all the way up to my chest with my hands.

I sent him an invitation as seductively as I could. Dan

grinned and said, "Come and fill me." He then knelt in front of me, where my clit was engorged and glistening, my pussy gaping wide open, and I felt my vagina opening to embrace his manhood.

Dan brightened, smiled, and gave me a tender glance before turning to face my waiting body. And he said, "Looks like you are pleased to see me." His voice almost made me pass out again.

I grinned and replied, "What a big cock you have."

He muttered, "All the better to love you with."

Not entirely in mock annoyance, I said, "Well, get on with it!" Dan then leaned over me and planted a kiss on my neck, breasts, and nipples. I was becoming desperate because I was becoming so turned on.

"Now!" I yelled, releasing my grip on my right leg and reaching out to grab his cock and pull it down into my eager vagina.

Dan mumbled. Then he began to slowly pierce me, saying, "That's an invitation I can't ignore." gradually going deeper and deeper while still gently dipping in and out. As he was doing it, I thought I was going to pass out from the intense cock that was filling me up and appeared to continue on forever. I also felt the head stop at the top of my vagina just as his pubic bone struck my clit and his balls my perineum.

I had never felt my cervix touched before, and it wasn't during a sexual encounter. I became aware that he had completely filled me, which triggered a fresh wave of feelings. I released my grip on my legs, which improved the balance of feelings by putting more pressure on my clit and less on my cervix.

Dan then pulled back about halfway, and I felt his cock's bell stroke that portion of my vagina where he had earlier pricked with his fingers. I felt like I had a g-spot even though I was unaware of it. Dan then began to slide back in, caressing my cervix rather than pushing it, till he was completely bottomed out then topped out. Then, in order to optimize the pleasure, he moved his hips, stimulating my clit, perineum, and cervix. I did the same.

Dan continued the pattern, a little faster this time. When I reached my peak again, I rocked to arouse myself even more and kicked out my legs, which were shaking wildly.

"Ohhhh, ooohhh, ooooohh, ahhhhh, aaahhhh, aaaaaahh."

Dan stopped rotating his hips as I cooed and began to work my nipples, which made everything even more intense.

"OHHhh, OOOhhh, OOOOOhh, AHHHhh, AAAHhhh, AAAAAAhh!"

I mumbled as I descended. "Please fuck me, fuck me hard, fuck me till you can fuck me no more!"

Dan looked up at me, then down at my body, which was spread out underneath him. Then he exclaimed, "Your wish is my command!" and began thrusting ever-faster.

These were still the lengthy strokes that hit my clit and slapped his tight balls against my perineum, together with the hip rock, which triggered my g-spot and cervix and sent me into yet another orgasmic wave.

My hips and legs swung to match the up-and-down, even-around rocking of my tits. The speed increased, and I was left in a state of constant ecstasy, orgasm after orgasm, my vagina spasming on his cock. I was surprised that he didn't come right away, as no man had ever given me so much pleasure in one sitting, far surpassing the games we had played earlier in the evening, which I had thought to be particularly special.

Dan's cadence altered to a series of long, hard strokes, and I felt his spunk—his hot, beautiful spunk—hitting my cervix, like it was attempting to flood my womb. Then, he growled. After giving me a few little thrusts till he was exhausted, he slumped on me after twitching once, twice, three, and four times. I began to cry tears of delight because everything was so lovely.

Dan turned to face me, though, and his voice was incredibly kind and compassionate. Tears welled up again. "Hey Babe, what's up? Did that hurt you?" Why did I say I was in love with a man I hardly know but thought I did and realized he had cared for me even when I was participating in a voluntary gangbang? "No, it was so, so good, the best, the very best I am so happy, so in love with you."

Whether it was the tears or something else, Dan's cock softened as he kissed them all away. He carefully got himself off of me and stated, "Grabbing a dressing gown," in an efficient manner. He left me laying in the center of his bed, completely euphoric and experiencing an orgasmic high I had never experienced before. "I need a drink after that, and I am sure you do, be right back."

I gently stroked my clit after feeling as though it were

throbbing. My pussy and vagina clenched as a result of that delicate touch, and I forced my fingers onto my sex. I either passed out or dozed off with my hand clasped to my pussy after having a series of excruciating spasms and moans.

Dan was coughing when I woke up, and I saw that he was standing there holding a tray. I could also see that there was another erection beneath the tray because he hadn't secured his dressing robe.

I spoke almost breathlessly. I quipped, "Wow, you seem happy to see me." "I can see what is below the tray, what's on it?"

Dan said, sounding amused. "I'm always pleased to see you; I heard you from downstairs, so I didn't know if you were alone."

I sulkily sighed. I grinned and teased, "I wasn't alone." "I had my thoughts of you and what you just did to me. But

I could do with that drink you promised, hot chocolate?"
My senses had detected it.

As soon as he placed the tray next to me, I realized how hungry I was since there were two plates with half of a lemon cheesecake cut into slices and two mugs of hot cocoa.

I tasted a bite of the hot chocolate, and it was delicious and almost gave me a spontaneous climax. I grabbed a slice of cheesecake and chewed into it. A food orgasm was something new for me, but then again, so much was new. Perhaps it was just my enhanced senses, but it was the meal of the gods and it made me shudder.

We talked about what they were like, the events of the evening, what we found appealing about each other, and what really turned us on while we sat there eating the cheesecake and sipping hot chocolate.

Dan kept talking about the wild rogering he had just given

me, so it's possible that nothing of significance—or perhaps everything—was known about each other outside of the bedroom.

Upon noticing that his erection was still visible, I excused myself for a moment and, upon returning from the bathroom, I reclined into the most open-legged position I could muster. Dan moved the tray from the bed to the floor, but he still had one slice of cheesecake left. However, as he turned around, he held it and put it to my lips, so I nibbled a little. He then sat down to suck off some of the cheesecake that he had smeared on both of my nipples with his other hand's fingers.

In spite of the amazing feelings, I was still able to extend my left arm and scoop up a generous portion of the topping with my fingers, which I then applied on his cock's bell. "Oh no, have a peek at it! I'll have to remove that." Dan slid back to provide me with more access, allowing me to lean forward and put him in my mouth while I laughed.

Even with the cheesecake, I was ecstatic about the sensuous experience because Dan's cock was enormous, firm, smooth, and had a salty and sweet pre-cum. All I had to do was try to put as much of it in my mouth as possible and use my tongue and lips to savor it. However, I couldn't handle even half of it, and I would need to talk to Bella about how much more I could take. I hope she and Alex are having a great time, crossed my mind momentarily.

Dan's hands were on my head, but they didn't feel like the porn that used to make me slam into him; instead, they were a soft patting and a suggestion that I should let him go. He lifted his head to kiss me deeply as I was doing it, and I felt him smear some of the topping over my labia. He sucked his fingers clean in a seductive manner when we broke up our kiss.

"Oh no, have a peek at it! I'll have to remove that." I didn't think the cheesecake had made it that far inside of me, but he swung around to lie head towards my feet so he could get his mouth on my pussy and take off the big amount of cheesecake from my lips before licking it clean.

It took me far too long to realize that Dan's position left me looking like he had a wonderful erection, but it was still there when I made the simple movement with my hand to get it back into my mouth. I sucked in as much as my skills would allow, then began to move my head back and forth while my hand cupped his balls, which had again grown into a large, firm bulge.

Dan's incredibly long fingers, which matched his cock, began to slip into my love tunnel as I felt it. He started with one, then to two, and then three, applying pressure up the front of my vagina and penetrating deep until there was a twitch as he went over my g-spot. Then he retreated once more, evoking a stronger response, and stepped outside, where the sensation intensified once again.

Dan's enchanted fingers continued to intensify the

experience, and to enhance the effect of his tongue and lips, he added a small movement with his thumb on my clit. I had to remove his cock from my lips in order to groan without running the risk of biting down on it because it was so hot. However, I continued to kiss the shaft and his velvety balls like the best pleasure, even sloshing up the enormous amounts of delectable pre-cum.

The intensity of his finger attack on me increased as he moved his left hand, which had been caressing my hip and butt, up my body and around to my breasts, where it found each tit and alternately tweaked the nipples. He briefly broke eye contact with me as he moistened his fingers with his hand and applied his slick fingers to my swollen nipples in an intensely sensual way.

All I could do now was grip his ass and sometimes sip the pre-cum nectar. I believe I passed out again when my orgasm tore through me like nothing I had ever experienced before.

"DDAAANNN!!!!     OHHHH!     AAAAHHH!!! Oooooooooohhh! AAAAah."I became aware that Dan was squatting between my legs and pointing his cock at me while I lay on my back. "Ready to be fucked Babe?"

I was eager as I gazed up at this attractive man, but I also wouldn't have denied him anything because he had given me so much love and pleasure. I grinned and nodded. He smiled back, then hoisted my legs straight up his torso, massaging them sensually as he did so. He then folded my calves over his shoulders.

He wrapped them around his chest with his left arm and placed his right hand around my waist before getting on his knees and pushing my butt off the bed. I felt his cock brush against my clit and along my lips. I needed him in me, so he softly rocked his hips to give me more clit massaging. It was almost too sensitive.

Even though I'm sure his magic cock would have made its

way into my yearning sex, I couldn't wait and pushed it down with my hand, getting a shallow penetration right away.

Dan gave me a downward glance, and when I nodded, he slid his hips forward, and I felt his body sink deeply inside of me until it touched my womb's entrance, causing me to gasp with delight.

Dan then retreated till I gasped and saw that the head of his cock was crossing my g-spot. At that point, Dan began penetrating me once again with a repeat of ecstasy. Then, while tenderly staring down at my body, he gently swayed me back and forth while using little strokes to intensify the sensation on my g-spot.

My body was rocking even if the thrusts were small since Dan was kissing my legs and simply supporting me on my shoulders. I fisted my clit with one hand while fiddling with my tits, which were causing my nipples to swell.

They were also rotating and moving up and down with an intriguing stimulation.

I quickly experienced another orgasm, and as it did, Dan carefully moved closer to try a deeper penetration. When it finally reached my womb, I let out a loud cry! I was on the edge of awareness again, writhing in ecstasy and uttering something I don't know.

"DDAANNN!!!!!      OOOOOO-AAAAAHHH!!!!! DDAAANNN!!!!    OMG!    Oooooooooohhh! AAAAhhhhhhhhh.

I remarked in a contentedly worn-out voice as I regained my attention and looked at the devoted face of the man who had given me more pleasure than I knew existed. "Make love to me, fill me with your seed, I need you so much." Slurring my words, though not as coherently as that.

I said, "But Dan didn't need any more encouragement," as

he eased me onto the bed and then released my legs, causing them to fall on either side of him. He began to pump his erection in and out of my sex with his arms on each side of me. He extended his tongue to flick at my nipples as they swung past his face, and they were long thrusts as he developed his rhythm.

His cock quickened the pace of his fucking as I caught my breasts and squeezed them together, allowing him to alternately suckle on my nipples. We continued to thrust at ever-increasing speeds until I experienced another orgasm.

"Aahhhhh, aaahhhh, aaaaaahh, Ohhhh, ooohhh, ooooohh, ahhhhh, aaahhhh, aaaaaahh."

And when I spasmed again, my hips shoved up as Dan's pelvis bucked and shook, forcing him to wait until I relaxed again, and I stretched my arms wide to grip for the sheets.

Whether it was that incident or just his sensing that it was the proper moment—which it was—Dan just began to beat me faster and faster while grunting like he was about to have an orgasm.

Then it arrived.

He sprayed my womb with burst after burst of hot spunk, followed by several brief thrusts and the pulsing of his member as my sex responded with its own spasms.

We shared a long kiss as though this was our last chance, and Dan skillfully turned us over so that I was lying on him and he was still inside of me. We gradually slowed down, came to a halt, and embraced.

I must have slept off because the next thing I recall is being snuggled into bed with Dan's body facing me. After that, I dreamed of being completely satisfied.

# Acknowledgments

The Glory of this book's success goes to God Almighty and my beautiful Family, Fans, Readers & well-wishers, Customers, and Friends for their endless support and encouragement.

# About The Author

I've spent nearly a decade penning romantic novels. As a passionate writer of erotica, I craft dark, romantic erotica. Anime Naked Truth Se of Sacred Sexuality: Forbidden Seducing Short Stories of an Erotica Nude Sexy Girl Poster. Alongside Erotic Mystery Fiction, Victorian Erotica Sex, Black & African American Erotica, Euthanasia, Daddy Teaching, Forced Domination, Alpha Monster Cuckold, and BDSM for Adults, there's an Erotic Fiction in Kinky Family. I write dark, sensual romance because I adore the power of darkness and everything that it entails. Romance novels have always been my favorite kind of books, and now I'm writing them. The idea that you will like reading and enjoying my fiction as much as I enjoy pushing the frontiers of sexual pleasure in my writing thrills me more than anything else.